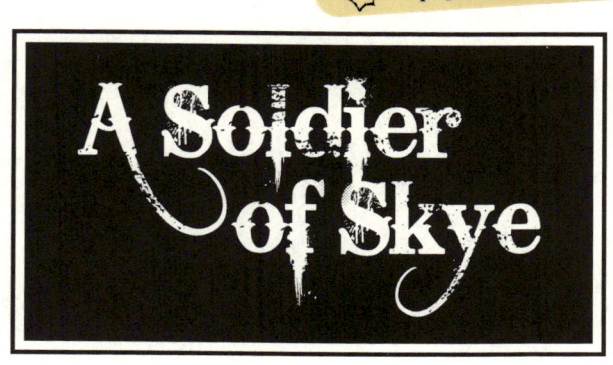

Lady Collette
enjoy my other
life:
"Growing old is mandatory
Growing up is optional

Gary Anderson
sams Dad.
11/26/56

A Soldier of Skye

being a
Wondrous Account
of
A Highland Soldier's

Adventures

in a

Magical Realm

by

Gary Anderson

AMBER SKYE
PUBLISHING

A Soldier of Skye © copyright 2014 by Gary Anderson. All rights reserved. No part of this book may be reproduced in any form whatsoever, by photography or xerography or by any other means, by broadcast or transmission, by translation into any kind of language, nor by recording electronically or otherwise, without permission in writing from the author, except by a reviewer, who may quote brief passages in critical articles or reviews.

ISBN: 978-0-9894003-4-3

Library of Congress Catalog Number: 2014937882

Printed in the United States of America

First Printing: July 2014

18 17 16 15 14   5 4 3 2 1

Cover and illustrations by Mike Foley Graphic Design
Edited by Patricia Duffield
Book Design by Chris Fayers

AMBER SKYE PUBLISHING
1935 BERKSHIRE DRIVE
EAGAN, MINNESOTA 55122
www.AmberSkyePublishing.com
ALSO ON FACEBOOK

Dedication

This collection of tales is dedicated to two extraordinary women. Kimberly Raths, Queen Katherine the Only . . . who was fair and fine as any sovereign in fact or fiction.

My mother-in-law, the late Marguerite Krautkremer, who listened to my stories without criticism but instead encouraged me.

Acknowledgements

It would be remiss of me to not acknowledge the people who have guided me along the convoluted path of the publishing journey: Judith Palmateer of Amber Skye Publishing and her associates Patricia Duffield, Kellie Hultgren, and Chris Fayers; Audrey McClellan, author of the "Eilean Dubh" series (www.Scottish Island Novels.com); Mike Foley of *Mike Foley Graphic Design*; and also Charles and Beth Knutson of MacGregor's Games; my wife, Gretchen, and my three children, Jennifer, Samantha, and Timothy; and to the men, women, and children, both past and present, of Clann Tartan.

Table of Contents

The Flower Bed
13

The Queen's Rose
19

The Urchin
25

The Women
30

Mari Harper
37

Treasures
47

The Gate
53

Bonny Glens
57

Koffay
61

Faces of the Clann
71

Rose and Thistle
75

Glossary
83

Author Biography
87

The Flower Bed

The moon was rising over the wooded hills to the east as mist was drifting slowly through the deserted festival grounds.

A minstrel walked up the hill to sit beneath the oak in the rock garden near the Scottish encampment.

He unslung the harp from his back, tuned it, and when he was satisfied, started playing. The music stopped and started as he struggled with its composition. And then, the mist, the moonlight, and the magic of the Autumn Equinox combined to form the music that started to pour from the strings of the harp.

Surely the soul of the minstrel controlled the melody, for it sang of old loves and the passing of the summer. As the music soared, the mist and the moonlight swirled and entwined to shape itself into the form of a woman. A princess of Faerie summoned by music, mist, and moonbeams. She was enthralled by the melody, and as each note shimmered in the air, she became a bit more tangible and less dreamlike. The Minstrel was mesmerized also. His fingers plucked the strings of their own accord, not by his direction. The music flowed, swelled and whirled, and wove a tapestry of enchantment in the night.

The Faerie Princess started to sing a counter-melody to the Minstrel's song. Her song was of new love and a new beginning. So the night hours sped by in a mystical wondrous haze for the two beings. The moon set, the music ceased, the Minstrel slept, and the Princess faded back into the silvery mist.

Every night of the festival, after the patrons were gone and the Blue Lion Tavern closed, the Minstrel returned to the oak on the hill and started to play the Song. The mist swirled, the moon rose, the Princess returned to sing her counter-melody, and just before dawn the Song would cease and the Minstrel would sleep.

As all things must, the Festival came to its end. The Minstrel walked up the hill for the last time and unslung his harp. He started the Song and the enchantment began again. Sensing the sorrow of parting in the Minstrel's song, the Princess reached out her hand and touched him for the first time. The touch turned to a caress and then a kiss. The Song changed to the music only lovers can know and hear. The moon set, the Minstrel slept, the mist dissipated, the Princess wandered and realized that she could never return to Faerie, for she had lain with a mortal. Desperately she searched for a place to hide, but the first cold frost of autumn seared her fragile beauty and she collapsed upon a gentle incline, just out of sight of the sleeping Minstrel.

With the dawn the Minstrel awoke, shouldered his harp, and left the Festival grounds, trying to remember and grasp the last fleeting images of a wondrous dream.

All of this happened many years ago during the first Festival in the Village of the Realm.

On a small rise just north of the Pavilion, you will find a bed of fragile blue and pink flowers. The grounds keepers say they have been there since the first Festival, but the landscape plan does not show any flower bed in that spot. The flowers bloom prettily every year during the Festival until the first frost of autumn, and then they wither.

During the late watches of the night, after the Autumn Equinox, I have heard, or perhaps I have thought I have heard, soft music being sung. It seems to come from the rock garden where the oak stands on the hill, near the Scottish encampment. It is a woman's voice that sings her sorrows over the hilltop, and sometimes, if the moon is up and the mist is rising, I can almost see a woman's form near the garden.

Ailean MacLeod Pvt.
Soldier Gaffney's Regt of Pike

The Queen's Rose

The Scottish soldier was enjoying the festival immensely. He had performed his guard and escort duties and was free for the rest of the day. And what a day it was! Soft winds, bright sun, laughing people and that clear crystalline air that only occurs in late September.

He was very nervous and excited that afternoon for he had in his hand a story. A wee bit of prose composed by himself. It was rolled into a cylinder and was tied with a blue ribbon with a spray of tiny pink blossoms entwined in it. The soldier was going to present this to the Queen.

Now dealing with royalty was an altogether frightening experience for the soldier. He had faced men armed with swords, pikes, axes and any amount of deadly devices without qualm, but the thought of speaking to the Queen made his palms sweat and his knees shake.

He had first seen her at the little Irish cottage called Ballina where she had sung a Scottish ballad for the people who had gathered there. He never thought that a queen could sing so beautifully, and to a group of common people besides. The soldier was captivated by her beauty and grace. He wanted to give her something to show her how much he thought of her. The only thing he had of any value was the little story he had written.

With a deep breath and sigh, he set out to present his poor gift to the Queen. The Queen was having tea with some of the courtiers and was being entertained by singers and minstrels. The soldier approached her, doffed his blue bonnet and knelt before her. The Queen bade him rise and asked his name and mission. He stammered his name and handed her his little bundle of prose and posies. He asked her to read it at her leisure, then bowing once more, the soldier withdrew from the royal presence.

The following morning during muster of the Scottish regiment, a lady-in-waiting asked for the soldier. He stepped forward out of formation and was presented with a beautiful yellow rose sent to him from the Queen. The soldier pinned the rose to his bonnet and proudly displayed this sign of royal favor.

That night the soldier marched out of the Village of the Realm with his regiment. It was time to start earning his money by serving in the wars. In time, the rose dried and withered.

The soldier unpinned the rose from his bonnet and carefully wrapped it in a cloth and stored it deep in his pack.

Years later the soldier's regiment returned to the Village of the Realm on their way home from the wars. As the soldier marched through the main gate, he felt warmth spreading out of his pack. He opened the pack, found the cloth that contained the rose, and opened it. The rose was still there, but it was no longer dry and faded. It was as full and fresh as the day it was first given to him.

Once again he pinned the rose to his bonnet, and once again he displayed the sign of royal favor. Once again he proclaimed his devotion to Katherine Stewart, "The Highland Rose."

The tale does not end here. It is still unfolding in the Village of the Realm, for not only does it speak of the magic of the Village but also of the love of a queen for her subjects, and, of course, the loyalty and devotion of a soldier.

If you should happen to find yourself in the Village of the Realm, look about. Perhaps you will see a Scottish soldier with a war axe slung over his shoulder and a beautiful yellow rose pinned to his bonnet, the very same rose of many years ago.

Ailean MacLeod Pvt.
Soldier Gaffney's Regt of Pike

The Urchin

I believe I first saw him many years ago, during my first visit to the Village of the Realm. I was down from Skye with a mercenary company recruiting fighting men for service in the Lowlands. The wines were sweet, the lassies were bonny, and the villagers were friendly. It was festival time for the Village of the Realm. Laughter and gaiety prevailed with minstrels and jugglers from more places than I ever knew existed.

I was examining some finely made shirts which were fashioned of cloth so smooth and in such a rainbow of colors that they would shame a peacock. There was a sudden movement behind a line of shirts and there he was.

He was a white-haired creature of six or seven years with laughing grey eyes and a dusting of freckles on his cheeks and nose. He grinned at me then spun about and with a flash of sun browned legs and bare dirty feet he vanished into the crowd.

Lads and lassies like him all look alike, whether in town or village, croft or common, but this one was disturbingly familiar. For the remainder of my stay in the village I looked for him to no avail.

Over the years and in subsequent stays in the Village, I would see the Urchin. Always when I would least expect it, he would appear with that impish grin and laughing grey eyes and then, miraculously, he was gone. I would catch a glimpse of him peering through a window at me or see his face in a looking glass in one of the shops. I would turn and he would scamper off mingling with the patrons. Who was he? Why did he haunt me so?

Every time I visited the Village during festival time, another peculiar question started to plague my thoughts. Didn't these people do ordinary everyday activities? It was true that I only visited in late summer and early fall. Other times of the year when I passed this way, I would not think of the Village until I had passed by the track that leads to it. I would always hurry straight on to my destination with nary a backward thought.

Although I had been to the Village a score of times in a like number of years, the Urchin always seemed the same age. I changed but he stayed the same, a lad of six or seven with white hair.

Last winter I was injured in a brawl with some Genoese crossbowmen. I was cut beneath my ribs. When the wound became inflamed, I lost my senses and slipped into delirium. I woke in a bed beneath the eaves of a building which had a window that looked out over a village green.

There, across the green, was a jousting track and the pavilion where I used to stand guard duty when the Village of the Realm was celebrating festival. A movement in the shadows, near the foot of my bed, caught my eye. The Urchin! He was grinning at me in that impish familiar way.

"Who are ye, lad?" I asked.

"Ailean, surely you have figured out who I am. A man as wise and widely travelled as you should know me."

"I confess that you have a certain familiar look about you, lad," I replied, "but I can't figure out why you are familiar."

"Ailean," he said, "I am you. I am the little boy inside of you that will never grow up. I am the spirit and excitement and wonder and pure joy of existing that lives within you. I am inside of you always, but only here in the Village of the Realm can I become tangible."

He gave me a wink and a grin. "It is the Magic of this place and this time that changes dreams and fantasy to reality. Ailean, you have been very close to death, and now you must return to your land of life and faded grey reality. We will speak together again, Ailean. You know where. Safe home, old friend."

Again I awoke. This time it was in my own vermin-infested bed in winter quarters in the Lowlands of Flanders.

I am recovering from my illness and am building up my strength. I will be leaving the Lowlands soon. I have to visit a little village far away. If I start in about a week, I should get to the village when the summer is waning and the Autumn Equinox occurs.

I'll sit in the shade beneath the grape vines at the Blue Lion Tavern and enjoy the jugglers and minstrels. Perhaps I'll steal a kiss from a saucy wench or a proud court lady and wait for a grinning white-haired lad of six or seven to sit down and talk to me.

Ailean MacLeod Pvt.
Soldier Gaffney's Regt of Pike

The Women

Morning in the Village of the Realm. The sun was slowly melting the stiffness out of my bones as the hot exotic beverage I was sipping dissolved the cobwebs of sleep from my mind. I was feeling every one of my many years of sleeping in the open. The many nights on rocks, grass, clay slopes and muddy river banks were catching up to me that morning. A mercenary's life is not all the enjoyment that the recruiting officers claim it is. Growing older is a somewhat painful and boring experience; however, it's better than dying young as so many of my friends and comrades had done. An old Scottish war wolf like myself shouldn't complain so much.

There I was on the last day of the festival in the warm sun with not a trace of the enemy about. It was a glorious morning, and I was sitting on the earth and stone stage that was called "The Bear." It was called "The Bear" because of the tree trunk that was carved into the shape of a huge bear, standing on its hind legs.

I believe that the bear wasn't really carved at all. My belief is that some type of magic was performed here to form the stage and the large animal it was named for. Those of you who are familiar with the Village of the Realm know that reality and fantasy walk hand in hand in this place, and often times they blend into something altogether unexplainable.

I noticed a splash of colors moving slowly towards me, drifting in and out of the groups of early morning patrons. And as the brightly hued bouquet approached, I realized that the colors were three women of extraordinary beauty.

One was wearing a gown of tawny silk with swatches of crimson, and another displayed a blend of sky blue, soft grey and white. The third was resplendent in a deep rich brown with streaks of russet flowing through the fabric. Never had I seen such an enchanting trio of women.

They were passing within a few yards of me when the woman in tawny and crimson with night-black hair stopped, looked directly at me, and said, "Good morn on ye, soldier. Are you by chance the Scotsman, MacLeod?"

"Aye, my lady," I replied. "I'm MacLeod."

The woman in brown smiled at me and said, "A white-haired urchin of six or seven years told us that if we wanted to see the festival that there be none better than Aileen MacLeod to be our guide and companion. What say you, brave soldier? Would you spend your day with us?"

Now I've been called a muckle of things over my lifetime, but stupid has never been my name.

"Of course, my ladies, I would be your escort gladly."

Once again the lady in brown spoke. "The first thing, MacLeod, is to call us by our names. I am Brianna. My cousin in tawny and crimson is Morgana, and my other cousin is Alana. Please use just our names and don't call us "my lady." We all four will be friends with no rank or social caste amongst us."

And so my beautiful bonny morning unfolded in the company of those three enchanting women and spread on through the afternoon. We cheered at the jousts and hooted at the patrons in the stocks. We threw vegetables at jeering lads and laughed at the entertainers on the Legend Stage. We sampled foods from Greece and the Holy Land, wines from the West Country, and ale from the local brewery.

We laughed at Morgana whose hands and face were greasy from the large drumstick she was eating. Brianna and Alana laughed even harder when Morgana wiped her hands in my beard and pulled me close to kiss my lips and transfer the grease from her face to mine.

They coaxed me to unsling my mandolin, and I sang and played for them a number of times during the day. The hours fled quickly by, and when Alana mentioned that Brianna had to start on a journey south, the tone of the day turned a wee bit melancholy.

Shadows were growing long and the air had a bite of cold in it when the three looked at each other and nodded their heads in agreement. Then, one by one, they stood on tip toe, hugged me and kissed me gently, murmuring something in my ear about being faithful friends forever, then turned and walked away.

The sadness of the parting paralyzed me for a while. By the time I started after them, they were half way up the big hill behind the Bakery Stage. I followed as fast as I could. When I reached the top of the hill, I saw them standing by the standards at the edge of the hill. The wind was rising, and the women lifted their arms as if to beckon the wind. They shimmered and seemed to ripple in the wind, and then they disappeared. Or did they? I saw movement down towards the trees near the riverbank. A cardinal and a blue jay flew into the evergreens, and above them, a wood thrush started south on her autumn flight.

Now in the long dreary hours of winter, I dream of the song of the wood thrush. In the mornings a blue jay calls high in the bare branches of a rowan tree. Her song is "aiee-aiee" or is she saying, "Ailean, Ailean," while a pretty tawny cardinal hops about in the bushes?

The magic of the Village of the Realm is at work again.

Ailean MacLeod Pvt.
Soldier Gaffney's Regt of Pike

Mari Harper

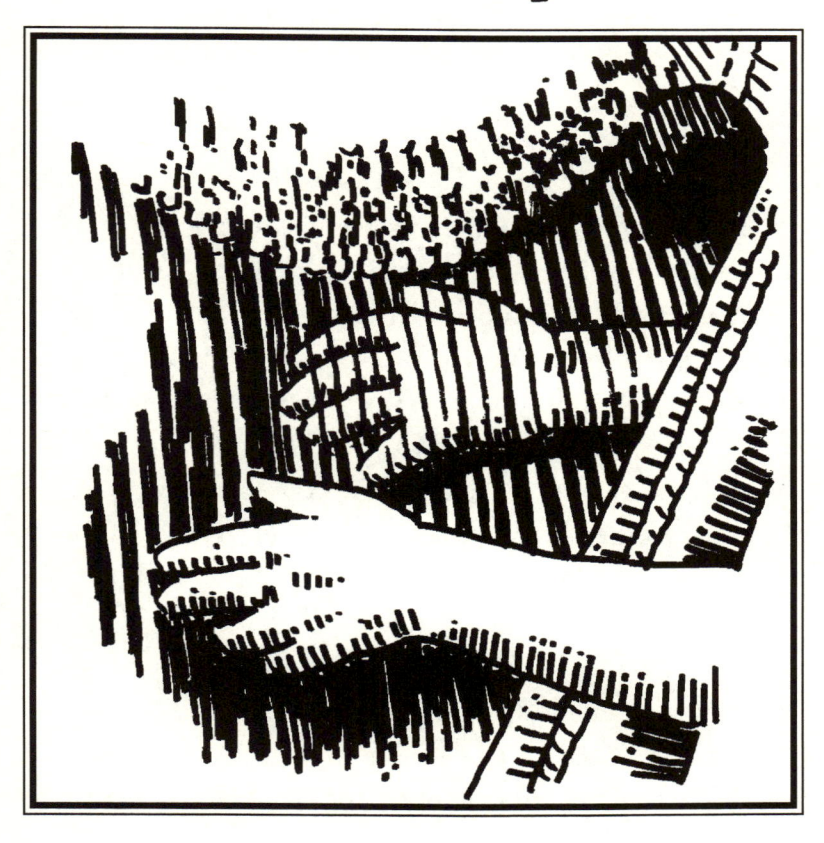

Mari was a slight willowy person with beautiful expressive eyes and short dark hair with glints of flame in it.

She was an excellent masterful harper who could enthrall all who heard her music. For many years I listened to her music at the Village of the Realm and enjoyed it immensely. However, in all those years I never heard her speak. Not one word.

One day I told a story to Mari about the yellow rose that I wear in my bonnet. As I told her, her eyes sparkled and she clapped her hands in appreciation and motioned to me to step closer. When I did, she unpinned the rose from my bonnet. She then opened a fine leather pouch which was worn on her belt and out of it took a clear tawny colored stone that was attached to a golden hook. She hooked the tawny drop on the rose and tied them both to the hollow sounding board of her harp. She then started to play.

The melody was unlike any I had ever heard. It was not of this world. The music brought memories of my childhood and fleeting images of a previous existence. But whose? Mine? Mari's? Another race of people?

I don't know how long I stood there or how long she played, but the music ended and

Mari gave me the tawny drop and pinned the rose back on my bonnet. Setting the bonnet on my head and the drop in my ear, I asked, "What was that all about?"

Mari ran her finger along the strings, creating a trill of rippling notes, and I heard a voice in my mind that replied "so you can hear me."

I stared completely dumbfounded. Again her voice said, "MacLeod, close your mouth or the swallows will nest in it."

"Mari, what did you do? What happened just now?"

The strings sang again and her voice said, "Tonight after moon rise meet me at the vine-covered wall near the waterwheel at the Hall of Scribes and all will be made clear."

I met Mari near the Hall of Scribes as asked. It was a soft night with fireflies winking in the shadows while the moon cast a silver benediction over the village. She sat on a bench and beckoned me to sit beside her. She uncased her harp and then began to pluck its strings. The voice sounded in my head once more and the story began:

I was a happy little girl many years ago, herding geese about my family's farm near a deep wood. One day the geese scattered into the wood, perhaps frightened by a fox. I tried to gather them together again. I searched and searched for my geese, but I could not find them. I was tired from searching and sat down in a shady glen to rest but for a moment. I did not notice the ring of mushrooms that encircled the little glen. I was very drowsy and fell asleep. When I awoke the glen had changed.

I had fallen asleep in a Faerie Ring and was now in the Land of Faerie. The trees were scarlet and golden in the autumn's bright apparel, and in that ring a multitude of Faeries and Elves clustered about me. They were smiling and their laughter was the sound of light silvery bells.

I was very frightened, no matter how friendly and pleasant the Faeries were. Then one elderly elf approached and gently took my hand. He smiled, nodded his head, and spoke in a sweet and reassuring manner.

"You'll do little one. Oh yes, you'll do very well."

I didn't know what he meant then, but later I would realize that from that time on I was to be a very blessed person.

The elf was named Gladeron, and he was a harpmaster, the finest harper of all of Faerie.

Gladeron walked me to the elven village where he lived. The village was a stand of huge trees whose trunks were hollow, and in those hollow trees the elves lived. Grottos of stone, moss and ferns provided shelter for the Faeries and Pisks that fluttered about on wings of transparent and varied hues.

Gladeron invited me in to sit and share a cup of honey and raspberry tea and a plate of sweet cakes. We talked about my lost geese and what would become of me when I returned home without them. It was then that Gladeron sadly said that I would not be returning to my home for a long time. By falling asleep in a Faerie ring, I would have to spend a thousand years in the Land of Faerie before I could return to my world. He was very comforting and reassured me that I would be happy in the Land of Faerie, and when I returned to my human world I would be a very special person.

The days passed and soon I was thoroughly immersed in my new existence. And in my new existence Gladeron instructed me to be a harper of elven tradition.

To become an accomplished harper in the art of elven harping, the apprentice harper must create his or her own harp. By creating the instrument a bond is forged between the harper and their instrument. Gladeron explained the process of bonding harpwood and a harper to me. Then Gladeron packed a knapsack with supplies, and together we walked into the woods to where the grove of harp trees grew. The journey took a day, and we set up a small camp on the edge of the grove at evening time.

Our camp was very cold, but Galderon explained that if we made a fire the Harp trees would become stressed. The next morning Gladeron led me to a large Harp tree. He asked me to put one hand on the tree trunk, which I did. He then placed one of his hands over mine and said, "Heart of Harp tree do you wish to bond with this young one?"

The tree shivered and a voice in my head said, "What manner of creature is this that begs a bond with me?"

Gladeron replied, "She is a young human that I would train and mentor as a harper if you would grant a bond with her."

The upper branches of the tree sighed with the passing of a gentle wind then the voice said, "Half way up my trunk is a branch for the bonding of human and harp tree. That branch misses the lark's song, and I believe it will sing very pretty as a harp."

Gladeron climbed the tree and located the branch with the abandoned nest. He secured the branch to a limb higher up the tree and proceeded to sever the branch from the Harptree trunk. He lowered the cut branch to the ground, and together we dragged the branch to our camp. Gladeron started trimming the branch and then cut it into three manageable lengths. Together we packed our camp gear and the three pieces of Harpwood and started our journey home.

When we arrived at the village, we hung the Harpwood lengths from the center beam in Gladeron's workshop so the resin in the wood could seep out and pool in a bowl set beneath it. In time a very small amount of liquid collected in the bowl. Gladeron put the bowl on the windowsill so the sun, moon and stars might cast their rays into the tawny colored resin.

Shaping the Harpwood pieces, carving, sanding, drilling, polishing, rubbing and molding, Gladeron and I made my harp. When I tired of the manufacturing process, Gladeron would instruct me by playing his own harp. I was taught finger exercises, string tones, runs and rills. We would then go back to making my harp.

It took forty human years to construct my harp and two hundred more to learn how to play it in the Elven fashion. Some days my fingers bled from practicing so long, and my blood seeped into the wood. My blood replaced the resin that had drained out of the wood from years before.

The drained resin that had been collected and saved was no longer liquid but a pliable substance that Gladeron instructed me to knead with my bloody fingers. In time the resin solidified, and Gladeron drilled a hole in it, and then inserted a golden harpstring into the hole and attached a golden hook to the harp string. There it was—a beautiful Harpstone ear drop. The ear drop was a blending of harper's blood, Harptree's resin and the magic of the sun, moon and starlight from the Land of Faerie. It was a marvelous talisman of magical translation.

My thousand years of training with Gladeron ended, and I was free to go back to the world of the humans. However, the cost of learning to be an Elven harper was leaving my physical voice back in the Land of Faerie. Every time I play my harp, my voice is heard back in that grove of Harptrees and in the Harpstone ear drop I have given to you. So you see, MacLeod, that is my story. I believe it matches well with your enchanted rose.

The night would soon turn to dawn, so Mari and I parted to get some rest for the last day of the Festival.

* * *

Mari stills plays her harp; however, she also is now making wondrous, magical jewelry, using the skills she learned in the other magical land.

Her most beloved creations are the ear drops. Look for her at festivals across the land. You will probably hear her harp singing close to where her jewelry is available beneath the sign of the Harpstone.

Ailean MacLeod Pvt.
Soldier Gaffney's Reg't of Pike

Treasures

The King and Queen were seated at the high table while the Courtiers were arranged to the right and left of the Royal couple. Visitors and Patrons were seated in orderly rows about the hall. Minstrels and Magicians entertained the assembly while tea and sweet cakes were consumed with great relish. The Queen's Tea was in progress and progressing nicely.

A Scottish Soldier walked slowly into the hall. As he walked, the black and yellow of his great kilt rippled and flowed. On his left hip was a basket-hilted backsword, on his right a large bone-handled belt dirk. A targe with a Celtic design was slung over his back and half concealed the war axe attached to his baldric. A sgian-dubh was tucked into the top of his right stocking, and he carried a murderous five and a half foot long sparth axe.

When the entertainers were finished with their music and magic, the soldier approached the High table. He removed his Blue Bonnet, which had a beautiful yellow rose pinned to it, and knelt to the royal couple.

"MacLeod," said the King. "Rise and tell us why you came fully armed into our presence."

"Where is your Mandolin?" asked the Queen. "You always sing and play for us."

"Please forgive me for wearing the tools of my trade in your Hall, as my Regiment will be leaving at sunset and my Mandolin and other personal effects are in the baggage train moving out of your Realm at this very moment. I would address the visitors who have come to share the bounty of the Realm, Your Majesties."

"Do so, MacLeod," said the King. And the Royal couple settled back to hear the words of the Scottish soldier.

"Assembled guests and visitors to the Realm, I am here to remind you that the Festival will be over at today's sunset. In a few short hours, King Henry, Queen Katherine, Lords and Ladies of the court and all of the denizens of this magic village will vanish into the mists of times gone by. I bid all of you to search for the treasures that are in this village. Gather them and hold them dear, for you may not pass this way again. I do not speak of the finery that is being sold in the village, but the jewels that are of the heart and soul of your very being. Seek these treasures as I have, and you will be rich beyond measure.

"I have found gold and silver in the innocent laughter of the children as they run and play about the festival grounds. That laughter will echo in my heart through the long days and nights ahead.

"Love is a jewel beyond price. Did you see the love in the eyes of the young people married here in the village during the Festival? The rich passion of young loves that contains all of the fire of a blood red ruby. Aye! Now there is a jewel of true beauty.

"There are couples here that have experienced all the joys and sorrows of a lifetime together. Their love is as deep and serene as the cool depths of a mighty emerald whose green calm bespeaks a comfortable love that transcends time.

"Now think of a magnificent topaz, warm and honey colored. Does that not remind you of the love of an old friend? A friend who knows all of your faults yet loves you in spite of them? The friend that senses your sorrows and comforts you when you haven't even cried out for help? Yes, I think a tawny golden topaz would represent an old friend's love.

"Have you ever pondered the blue of the sky on a September morning? A sparkling clear blue that promises an exciting eventful day that leaves you tingling in anticipation. That, my friends, is a sapphire. The sparkle of a stranger's eye as they laugh and joke with you while in line at one of the booths. Perhaps one of the mimes or minstrels smiles at you, or an old Scottish soldier winks at you. That sudden little glint of shared delight with a stranger, to me, is the star buried in a blue sapphire.

"'Tis said that the rarest of all the world's gemstones is a diamond. It is difficult to find but worthy of the search. I believe that you will find your diamond where and when you least expect it. It will appear to you for only a moment, and you must be ready to claim it when it appears for the chance may never come again.

"I have found my diamond. The jewel will warm my heart and illuminate my soul in the dark dreary days of the coming winter."

The Scottish soldier leaned over the high table, reached out and brushed the Queen's cheek with his hand, and there on his finger was a shimmering drop of crystalline moisture.

"A Queens's tear," said the soldier as he touched the tear to his lips. "Lords and ladies go forth to find the treasures of which I spoke and think kindly of those of us who dwell in this magical village. If in the coming year you desire to see us, just close your eyes and search us out beyond a sweet dream and a beautiful memory."

The Scottish Soldier bowed low to the King and Queen and to the assembled guests. Then with a swirl of his great kilt, he strode out of the hall into the past.

Ailean MacLeod Pvt.
Soldier Gaffney's Regt of Pike

The Gate

The moon was a silvery coin shimmering in the sea of night. Clouds raced through that sea like gossamer galleons on a voyage to distant lands. Night breezes laughed and chased each other through the oak boughs and played hide and seek about the garrets and gables of the village before they scrambled up the walls and vaulted off the battlements of the main gate.

I walked the nearly deserted streets and lanes of the darkening village and allowed the night to soften the sharp sword edge of reality and turn it to a gentle caress of sweet memory. The Festival was over. The patrons were gone. Just a few of the dreamers, like me, were left to wander the village and breathe in the rapidly fading magic that is the Village of the Realm.

Ah! The magic! To a young patron, the magic is new tastes, sights, sounds, and characters from strange and exotic places. To their parents, it is the delight and the excitements in their children's eyes as new experiences are explored. For the older patron, perhaps these sights and sounds revive the dreams they had when they were very young. Dreams that were created by stories told to them by long gone friends and family members. Yet for some, it is the return to their dreams and fantasies that quickens the magic.

The structures in this village have a certain timeless look about them. They are set against hills, rocks, and trees, like they just grew there. And perhaps they did just sprout up out of the earth. It wouldn't surprise me at all if they did. However, now the magic is fading rapidly as the last of the inhabitants leave the village. For you see, the real magic lives in the hearts of the creatures and folk of this realm. From the King and Queen to the scullery lads and serving wenches. From the lords and ladies to the rat catcher and the grave digger. From the dancing girls, jugglers, shop keepers and street hawkers to knights in armor, right down to a Scottish mercenary like myself, in worn leather boots, threadbare moth-eaten great kilt, and four hundred years' worth of wrinkles in my face. Together we bring the realm to life for young and old alike.

As I walk the grounds, I wonder if this is my last time ever in the Village of the

Realm. For some it is. Some will never stroll these streets or gaze on these buildings again. If I should be one of those who will never return, I have at least these memories and this wee glimpse of a wondrous Realm to last me forever. I walk down the lane past Bad Manor, a place of feasts and revels for villagers and patrons alike. To the right are the jousting track and the pavilion that held countless seasons of combat and feasting. I continue up the hill to where the Scottish encampment once stood and past the vine-covered crofts and stables now all empty, their magic departing with the folk of the Realm. I pass the bawdy Blue Lion Tavern, once bursting with boisterous, raucous patrons; and on my left, Folkstone Hall, always full of crafts and music but now shuttered. One last look back, as the moon silvers the roof lines and the oaks, while the night breezes say, "No, don't leave us." Then I'm through the gate.

Silean MacLeod Pvt.
Soldier Gaffney's Regt of Pike

Bonny Glens

The mountains were high. The waves
went rolling by.
The miles seemed to stretch on endlessly
and more. We marched and we cried,
we struggled and we tried to forget
the bloody horror that is war.
Oh Great God, tell me when will I see
the bonny Glens that I roamed and loved
as a lad. The farther that I roam the more
I miss the hills of home and the waters
of the Carron and the Bran

Do the women of the glen miss their hieland
men? Do they see their eyes and kiss their
lips at night in dreams? Do they pray to
the stars, to Venus, and to Mars to protect
their clansmen on the battle scene.
Oh Great God, tell me when will I see
the bonny Glens that I roamed and loved
as a lad. The farther that I roam the more
I miss the hills of home and the waters of
the Carron and the Bran

The lads that I knew are all so very few
since we left the hieland hills that we
loved so well.
Blades found their nests deep within my
comrades' breasts. I nee'r again will hear
they're hieland yells.
Oh Great God, tell me when will I see
the bonny glens that I roamed and loved
as a lad. The farther that I roam the more
I miss the hills of home and the waters
of the Carron and the Bran.

The linnet and the deer, the streams
a'flowing clear. The bracken and the heather
smelling clean and neat.
The smiles and the sighs and the sky
blue Scottish eyes. The kisses from her
lips so warm and sweet.
Oh Great God, tell me when will I see
the bonny glens that I roamed and loved
as a lad. The farther that I roam the more
I miss the hills of home and the waters
of the Carron and the Bran.

Koffay

The angry grey clouds were spilling cold grey rain on the cobbles and stones that were the fabric of the dismal grey town.

I was cursing myself for leaving my warm, dry billet back on the continent to be walking cold and wet in this miserable town on the West Coast of Scotland. Now don't get me wrong, I love the Highlands and the Scottish Isles, but this filthy pile of rocks is one part of my home country that is best ignored, or better yet, forgotten.

I had accompanied my Company Commander, Captain Munro, to this town after leaving our regiment in the Low Countries. We were under orders to raise additional fighting men to fill out the regiment. Our losses from battle were low; however, we were at about seventy percent strength due to disease and desertion. We hoped to recruit ten to fifteen score men to bring us back to full strength.

I was sloshing along an alley in the meaner part of the town when I heard my name called out.

"MacLeod?"

I looked about quickly and saw an old woman sitting in a doorway trying to escape the pelting rain.

"What do you want? Do I know you?"

"You did once, MacLeod," she said. "You sang a sweet love song to me on a bright autumn afternoon."

She was daft. She had to be. I had never been in this town before, and I would never sing any song to this old creature.

"You must have mistaken me for someone else, old mother. I have never seen you in my life."

"You are mistaken, MacLeod. That afternoon you were wearing a red great kilt with a coarse black shirt and blue and yellow brassards around your sleeves. You had a shiny breastplate on, and you played a mandolin and sang like a bird. Well, like a raven with a chest cold, but it was a bonny song none the less. And you had a beautiful yellow rose pinned to your bonnet."

That statement about the rose stunned me, for you see, I only wear the rose at a little village far away and only for the few days when the village celebrates its festival. I had to question this woman about this song and village business.

"Old woman," I said, "we are going to drown in this rain. Come, and I will take you to the inn where I am presently lodged, and we will speak of this matter further."

She struggled to stand. When she was upright, she clutched my arm to her side, and we started on down the hill to my inn like a pair of crabs scuttling through the incoming tide.

The Rose and Thistle was a middle-class inn that catered to a quiet, reserved clientele that enjoyed clean rooms and excellent fare. Bawds and doxies were not welcomed there. Obviously the Captain picked these quarters. I would have selected something a wee bit livelier. I hurried the old woman through the common room, thankful that there was no one about to see us. After hurrying down a passage to a small private dining room, we entered and I quickly shut the door.

A fire was crackling on the hearth, spreading warmth and a sense of ease and comfort into the small room. I glanced out of the window where there was a small garden being slowly pounded into a grey, oatmeal-like consistency by the rain. That was on the other side of the leaded panes. On this side, all was dry and cheery. I sprawled out on the settle near the fire while the old woman perched on a low, three-legged stool on the other side of the hearth from me.

"Now, old mother," I said. "What do you mean when you speak of me singing to you, and a bright red rose on my bonnet?"

"Oh, MacLeod, you are such a simpleton. I was at the Village of the Realm a single month past. I heard you sing to the Queen twice during her teas, and I watched your Company go through pike and sword drills down by the Bear Stage. And the flower you were wearing on your bonnet is a yellow rose."

The old woman had me alright. She must have been at the Village, but I would have remembered singing to her. Perhaps I had sung to someone else and in her old demented mind she thought the song had been for her. Yes, that would explain it.

The old woman was scurrying about the hearth and had taken something out of a sack that was buried in the folds of her black garments. She dropped whatever it was into a kettle of water and then suspended the kettle over the fire. She sat back down on the stool, shook herself a bit, like a small black hen on its nest, and she said, "Do you remember a woman with long black hair and blue eyes? She was wearing a black velvet gown with ivory brocaded panels in it and a scattering of seed pearls about the bodice and shoulders? You sang to her on Shepherds Green near the Irish Cottage."

"Why yes, I remember her quite well. As bonny a lady as I've ever seen."

The old woman looked at me with piercing blue, almost violet, eyes and said, "I was, or more to the point, I am that woman."

Aye and pigs nest in the tops of rowan trees. She was daft. She couldn't be serious, although she had a convincing way about her.

"While ye get your wits about you, MacLeod, allow me to share something special with you."

And with that, she took two earthen cups from the mantle and filled them with the contents of the kettle that she had put over the fire a few minutes back. She handed one cup to me, and then settled back on her stool, clutching the other cup in both of her birdlike hands. Then the aroma of the liquid in my cup enveloped me, and I was transported away to the Village of the Realm.

Koffay, I believe it is called. An exotic beverage brought to Europe by the Venetians. I would drink pints of it in the Village. That was the only place I had ever tasted koffay. The taste and smell brought to mind clear sparkling mornings and laughing happy people celebrating festival. What wonderful memories this drink recalls.

"MacLeod," she said, "everyone in the village knows of your rose. They know it was given to you by the Queen and how it withers and dies when you leave the village. Everyone also knows it blooms as fresh and full as ever when you carry it back into the village. MacLeod, it is much the same with me. The magic works on people if you believe in it. Haven't you noticed how bright and gay everyone is when they enter the village? And how tired and drained you are when you leave?

You know more than most about the Village Magic, MacLeod. Can you doubt what I am saying to you?"

No, I could not doubt a thing she told me. I knew it was all so true. Over the years, I had experienced so much of what some people call magic in that little village. Enchantments, fantasy, dreams, magic? I stopped doubting long ago. Now, I believe and accept the unbelievable.

The old woman and I talked and reminisced at length about people and occurrences in the Village of the Realm, and then I must have dropped off to sleep. Suddenly I was being shaken rather roughly and came close to sliding off the settle and onto the floor.

"Wake up, Ailean, and start packing. We're leaving for Skye in the morning. I want to see if we can enlist some of your clansmen into the regiment. Of course, I want them to be at least half your age and half again as ornery as you are, Greybeard."

"Aye, Captain. I'll start packing now and make arrangements for transport."

I looked about the room quickly. The old woman was gone. The cups were back on the mantle. The kettle was sitting on the hearth, away from the fire. Did I dream this? Was my mind slipping?

"Ailean, have you been entertaining women in here today? Look what I found under the stool near the hearth. An earring, and a most unusual earring at that. It's a teardrop-shaped pearl set in silver with seed pearls around it. I seem to recall seeing earrings like this before. Last month in the Village of the Realm it was. On a raven haired woman with blue, almost violet, eyes. You know, Ailean, I could almost swear I can smell koffay. Do you remember that drink from the Village?"

"Aye, Captain, I can taste it still."

Ailean MacLeod Pvt.
Soldier Gaffney's Regt of Pike

Faces of the Clann

In days long ago as a much younger man,
I joined a fighting company of braw pike
men. From hielands and the lowlands and
the isles to the west from Wales and
from Erin we recruited all the best.

We sailed o'er the North Sea, how our
songs did ring. The pipes they sang sae
bonny when we joined the Swedish King.
With our pikes upon our shoulders and a
sword for every man, our tartans were a
litany of all the fighting clans.

Our leader was an Irish laird, Gaffney was
his name. We had Seamus and Nowack
and Black Dougal MacLain. Sargeant
MacGregor with Hellish Elish, too, and
a pack of MacLeods from the Isle of Skye
to sweeten up the brew.

We had Cameron and Thorne and Loric
MacStier. We had Rowan and his daughters
with hair like living fire. Ferguson and Cauley,
Ian and MacKinnon, big Matta MacLain, and
sweet Helspeth McClellan.

As I sit by my fire and I dream of the years.
The laughter and the sorrows the joys and the
fears. Life, it was much sweeter in that far
off German land. In the embers of my fire
I see the Faces of the Clann.

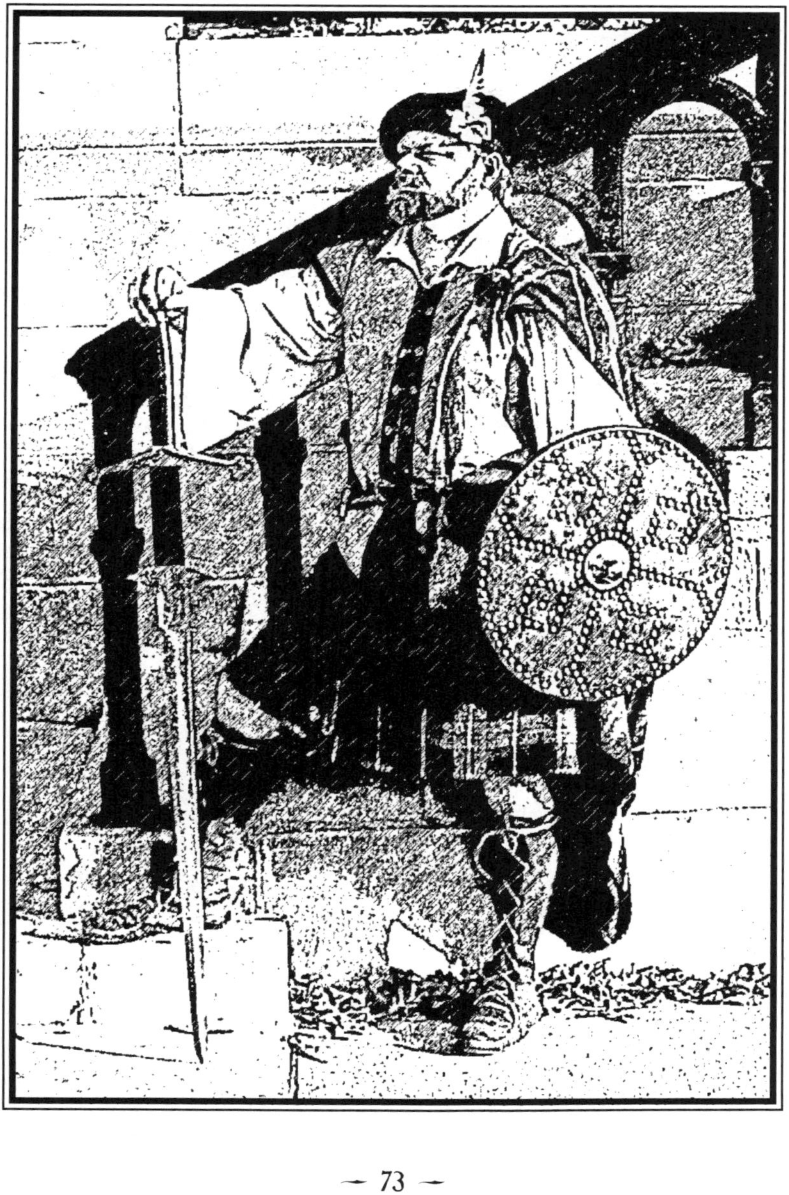

Rose and Thistle

I had known Ailean MacLeod for many years. He enlisted with Gaffney's Regiment of Pike a year after I did. I taught him how to tan hides and make a targe. He taught me songs and how to play a mandolin. We stood shoulder to shoulder in the pike line, and fought back to back, covering each other when our line broke and the battle turned into a melee. We marched together through Pomerania and drank our way through all of Scotland. Finally, we settled down to a less active profession—tanning. We were too old to continue the Military life, so we set up a small tannery near Loch Dunvegan on the Isle of Skye.

MacLeod had been born near here, and the passing of the years had erased the problems that had caused Ailean to flee Skye so many years ago. We celebrated the New Year in the usual way, Airing of the Plaids in the morning and first footing in the afternoon and evening.

Airing of the Plaids was a colorful celebration. We hung our kilts and all matter of tartans on the bushes and in the lower branches of the trees around the village. It was a bonny show. Let the wind and cold air blow through the fabric, cleansing and freshening the wool.

First footing consisted of visiting all the homes and crofts that we could, eating, drinking, visiting, and gossiping along the way. No one visited our cottage by the tannery, due to the smell of the tanning pits, so Ailean and I traveled about visiting. The odor of the pits had impregnated our clothes and no amount of airing or cleaning ever completely destroyed the smell.

We were welcomed at all the cottages in spite of the odor. I think it had something to do with the two large jugs of whisky that I carried and the mandolin that was slung over Ailean's shoulder.

The common room in the Inn was ringing with joy and celebration well into the night. Ailean and I had regaled the crowd with songs and stories of our travels as pikemen with a mercenary group during the German wars. Ailean liked to talk about the little Village of the Realm we had visited that seemed to exist only during the late summer and early fall, and the beautiful woman that reigned there as its Queen.

He took a dried out rose from his pack and told the people that it was given to him by the Queen and would bloom again whenever he walked back into the little village. I knew it was true, for I had actually witnessed it in the past. The listeners laughed and said we had breathed too many fumes from the tanning pits, or, more likely, from the whisky I had brought.

A storm had blown in from the sea in mid-afternoon and had whistled and piled snow about the village. By midnight, the snow had stopped and the sky was clearing to reveal the stars and a full winter's moon. Ailean said he was going to go outside for a while to clear the whisky from his head. I knew better though. He would often sit and gaze at the full moon with the same longing and subdued passion of a Highland wolf. I believe that, for some reason, the full moon conjured up visions of the little, far away village for Ailean. Before he left, he hung his mandolin carefully on a peg near, but not too near, the Inn's fireplace, then weaved out through the revelers, into the night.

I awoke the following morning with a throbbing skull and a terrible taste in my mouth. When I stood, the floor in the Inn rolled like the waves on the sea, and I had to clutch the counter under which I had spent the night.

Angus MacCrimmon, the Innkeeper, was woefully surveying the damage to his establishment. "Good day, Angus." I said. Angus just grunted at me. I looked about the Inn and asked, "Where's MacLeod?"

"I haven't seen him since last night, Sean. Perhaps he found a young lass who wouldn't have minded having old age creep up on her to celebrate the New Year."

While the situation was possible, I doubted it. "Ailean left the Inn last night in one of his strange moods. He usually shuns other people altogether when he is like that," I said. "Perhaps we had best go look for the old fool, Angus. It was a cold night, you know."

We searched the village and many crofts, to no avail. We walked down the track to the tannery when I thought of the ruins above the loch. Some say the ruins were a watchtower or a beacon. I don't know what they are, other than old. A place like that would appeal to MacLeod. It was away from people and would have an unparalleled view of the loch, the hills, and the winter moon.

Angus and I started up the winding path to the hilltop where the ruins lay. When we were half a bow shot from the ruins, I saw the yellow and black of Ailean's plaid—the unmistakable colors of Clan MacLeod.

We hurried up and around to where the ruins lay. There in the lee of a small wall was MacLeod. He was half sitting, with his legs straight out in front of him and his hands tucked into the folds of the great kilt. His face was calm and composed. It appeared that the wind, which had swept the ruins of snow, had also swept the lines and years from his face, revealing a younger, happier, more serene person than I had ever known. So this was the end for an old Scottish war wolf. To die while looking out over Loch Dunvegan, on a cold clear night, beneath a full moon, was all an old soldier could ask. It was much better that lying in a cramped cottage in your own stink, with nary a glimpse of the sky to free your spirit.

I couldn't look at my old friend for a minute. It seemed that the wind up there stung my eyes and made them water a bit. "Sean, look at this," said Angus. I turned back and looked. Angus had pulled back the folds of MacLeod's great kilt to reveal Ailean's hands. There, clasped lovingly in the cold lifeless grip, was a rose, a beautiful yellow rose, in full bloom, entwined with a purple Scottish thistle. Then I understood why MacLeod looked so happy and contented. After all those long years, he had finally left, to take service with his Queen in a little village far away.

Sean Cawley Pvt.
Soldier Gaffney's Regt of Pike

Glossary of Terms

Baldric: A belt worn over one shoulder and used to carry a weapon or sword or other implement

Basket Hilted Back Sword: Traditional Scottish sword, with a basket to protect the hand, sharpened on the cutting edge of the blade; top of blade is flat with no edge

Bawds: Women in charge of brothels

Billet: Military term for assigned position/post

Blue Bonnet: Traditional Scottish cap

Bonny: Scottish term for attractive, nice or pretty
Bran: A river in the central highlands of Scotland
Brassard: Ribbon(s) worn around biceps to mark the rank of a military man
Braw: Handsome, brave, manly
Breast Plate: Piece of armor worn over the chest
Caste: Social rank
Croft: Small rural home or farmhouse
Carron: A river in the central highlands of Scotland
Common: Communal ground, village green
Dirk: Scottish belt knife
Doxies: A lover or mistress
Galleon: Large three- or four-masted sailing ship
Hielands: Highlands
Isles of the West: Scottish Inner and Outer Hebrides
Koffay: Coffee
Lee: Leeward, opposite of windward, sheltered
Linnet: A common European singing bird

Litany: A prayer or list of articles

Loch Dunvegan: Lake Dunvegan/Dunevegan Castle; clan stronghold of the Clan MacLeod

Mandolin: A small relative of the lute in use during the 16th century to the present

Muckle: In Scottish Gaelic means many or alot

Pisks: A pert, cheeky pixie or child

Pomerania: Northern Germany and Poland

Rowan: Tree in Europe. Known as Mountain Ash in North America

Sae: So

Score: A unit of measure equaling 20. Therefore ten to fifteen score equals 200-300

Sgian-dubh: Translates as "Black Knife" and is tucked into the top of a Scots' right leg stocking

Skye: Island in the Hebrides. Loch Dunevegan is on Skye

Sparth Axe: A long handled axe with a crescent blade whose lower point is attached to the handle providing a grip for the hand—length is approx five feet

Stocks: A timber frame used for confining the arms and legs. Used for punishing petty offenders

Swedish King: Gustavus Adolphus II Hired 20-30 thousand Scottish soldiers to fight in the Thirty Years War

Talisman: An object that exerts magical or occult power

Targe: A round shield eighteen to twenty-two inches in diameter. Usually Oak wood which is 1/2 inch thick. Covered with leather and decorated with metal studs, or tacks, in Celtic designs

Gary Anderson is a Vietnam U.S. Navy Veteran, musician, composer, artist and, most importantly, a husband and father. As a musician, he has shared his musical talents of Mandolin and Tenor Banjo with a Dixie Land band at the Minnesota State Fair, Renaissance fairs, coffee houses, bars/pubs, civic festivals and countless jam sessions. He has also enjoyed his time working as a living historian at Murphy's Landing, Old Fort William, Big Island, Eagle Creek. He has also participated in re-enactments of English Civil War Battles at Fort Creve Cour, in Peoria, Illinois, and at The Museum of American Frontier History in Staunton, Virginia.

Gary lives in Bloomington, Minnesota, with his wife and two granddogs.